SEAGULL SiD
and the Naughty Things His Seagulls Did!

DISCARD

SEAGULL SID
and the Naughty Things His Seagulls Did!

Dawn McMillan

Illustrated by
Ross Kinnaird

DOVER PUBLICATIONS, INC.
Mineola, New York

We'll tell you the story of Seagull Sid,
and the naughty things his seagulls did
to reclaim what gulls had owned before
people came to the sandy shore!

These people brought boats, and surf skis fantastic!
But they littered the beach with cans and plastic,
then lay on the sand, row upon row,
with tummies and bottoms up for show!

With radios blasting the quiet sea air,
with barbecues, picnics and food everywhere!
While the gulls stood hunchback, quiet and dumb,
waiting for someone to throw them a crumb.

"Enough!" said Sid, one sunny Sunday.
"Come, my friends, we'll chase them away.
"Time to be rid of this intruder called Man!
"Let's get together and think of a plan."

A grand plan they agreed on, simple and clear.
Sid strutted with pride — it was all his idea.
The seagulls stood tall and fluffed up each feather.
"Ready?" squawked Sid. "Let's do this together!"

They took off in convoy, all flying low.
Sid took the lead, the first one to go ...

s-p-l-a-t

on the hat of a picnicker below!

There was the picnic,
all ready to eat.
"Bombs away!"
Sid led the fleet.

Bullseye on the
apple pie!

No mistake on
the chocolate cake!

Plop! Slop!

Then special assignments for a chosen few;
tricky tasks for skilled gulls to do.

What a team: Kit, Jan, Howell, Jack,
Jim, Bob, Dot and Chris ...
Working together with only one miss!

And then there was Freda,
with potential as leader,
but they didn't need her ...

Because,
with a scurry and flurry,
the people left in a hurry!

Drivers in cars, anxious to go,
boats and surf skis all in tow.
Picnics abandoned, no radio.

Sid and his mates all gathered round
the remains of a picnic, there on the ground.

A victory feast, but first the speeches.
"Yes! Seagulls *will* take back the beaches!"
Applause for Sid as he squawked in praise
of his seagulls' courage and winning ways.

"Thank you, team," Sid cried out loud.
"You were right on target! I'm so proud!
"Splat attacks with such precision!
"Of course, I made the right decision!"

"I used my plan. It was a winner.

"And now, my friends,
you may eat your dinner!"

About the author

Dawn McMillan lives in Waiomu, a small coastal village on the western side of the Coromandel Peninsula in New Zealand. She lives with her husband, Derek. Dawn writes lots of different things: fiction and nonfiction, poetry, stories for school readers, and picture books. Sometimes her work is serious; sometimes it's just for fun. This one is just for fun.

About the illustrator

Ross Kinnaird is an illustrator and graphic designer. He lives in Auckland, New Zealand. When he's not illustrating a book, or being cross with his computer, he enjoys most activities to do with the sea. He loves visiting schools to talk about books and drawing and has been known to draw really funny cartoons of teachers!

Bibliographical Note

This Dover edition, first published in 2019, is an unabridged republication of the work originally published by Oratia Media Ltd., Auckland, New Zealand, in 2012. This book is copyright. Except for the purposes of fair reviewing, no part of this publication may be reproduced or transmitted in any form or by any means, whether electronic, digital, or mechanical, including photocopying, recording, any digital or computerized format, or any information storage and retrieval system, including by any means via the Internet, without permission in writing from the publisher. Infringers of copyright render themselves liable to prosecution.

International Standard Book Number

ISBN-13: 978-0-486-83247-0
ISBN-10: 0-486-83247-3

Manufactured in China by RR Donnelley
83247301   2019
www.doverpublications.com